ell, Cece, author, aillustrator.
hick and Brain. Smell my foot!

)19
3305248227807
a   07/01/20

Chick and Brain
Smell my Foot!

Cece Bell

CANDLEWICK PRESS

CONTENTS

Chapter 1
Foot

12

That is much better!

Now I will smell your foot.

SNIFF!

14

Chapter 2
Spot

19

Chapter 3
Lunch

40

45

48

Chapter 4
Other Foot

You did?

Yeah. I *know* I did.

Look. Spot said that your foot smelled like chicken.

Yes. That was nice. Spot made me feel good.

Then he invited you to lunch.

Yes. That was nice, too. Spot made me feel special.

No! No, no, NO!

I know that Spot is a DOG!

Yes. I know that, too.

Do you know what dogs eat?

Dog food?

Yes! And chicken! And chicken *feet*!

So if a dog tells you that your foot smells like chicken, you better WATCH OUT!

Mmm . . . chicken foot.

66

Look, Jerry Kalback, look!
This book is for you.

First edition 2019

Library of Congress Catalog Card Number 2019938941
ISBN 978-0-7636-7936-1

20 21 22 23 24 CGB 10 9 8 7 6 5 4 3 2

Printed in Mankato, MN, U.S.A.

This book was typeset in JHA My Happy 70s.
The illustrations were created in watercolor and ink.

Candlewick Press
99 Dover Street
Somerville, Massachusetts 02144

visit us at www.candlewick.com